KU-428-783

SPIDER AND HIS SON FIND WISDOM

Obi nkyerekyere nyansa kotoku mfa nkɔto adakam mmegyina
adihɔnse se, "Kyere me asem!"
No one should gather wisdom in a bag, put it in a box,
then stand on a road and say, "Teach me wisdom!"

—Akan proverb

Schools Library and Information Service
S00000155711

With thanks to Scott and Henry for sharing their nyansa and love
—M. L.

For John, my wise son
—C. R.

Spider and His Son Find Wisdom is based on "How Wisdom Became the Property of the Human Race" from *West African Folk-Tales* by William H. Barker and Cecelia Sinclair. London: George G. Harrap & Company, 1917. This tale is from the Asante and Fante peoples of the Akan culture of Ghana.

Copyright © 1998 by The Rourke Press, Inc.
Illustrations copyright © 1998 by Charles Reasoner.

Published by Troll Communications L.L.C.

All rights reserved. No part of this book may be reproduced or utilized in any form or by any means, electronic or mechanical, including photocopying, recording, or by any information storage and retrieval system, without written permission from the publisher.

Published by arrangement with The Rourke Press, Inc.

First paperback edition published 1999.   ISBN 0-8167-6327-5

Printed in the United States of America.

10 9 8 7 6 5 4 3 2 1

PRONUNCIATION AND DEFINITION GUIDE

Twi (CHWEE) is the language of the Asante people of the Akan (AH kahn) culture of Ghana.

Ananse (Ah NAHN seh): the main trickster in stories of the Akan culture.

Aso (AH soh): Ananse's wife.

calabash (KAL uh BASH): a vine and its gourd.

denden (DEN DEN): loud.

kente (KEN teh): a handwoven regal cloth made by the Akan.

kokuroo (Koh KOO roo): huge.

Ntikuma (N tik OO mah): Ananse's son.

nyansa (Nie AHN sah): wisdom.

paw or **pɔw** (PAW): to bump.

pem so (PEM SOH): to bump.

tetsee (tes EE): a descriptive sound.

DUDLEY PUBLIC LIBRARIES
L   43893
155711   5a
J398.2 AFR

SPIDER
AND HIS SON FIND WISDOM

An Akan Legend

Retold by
Melinda Lilly

Illustrated by
Charles Reasoner

Troll

Long ago, when the world was starting to learn about itself, there lived a spider named Ananse. This big-headed fellow wove his sticky, tricky webs across the villages of West Africa. Ananse told everyone he was unusually big-headed for a spider because his head stored nyansa—all the wisdom in the world.

One day in the bustling marketplace, as Ananse advised the weaver of the best patterns for kente cloth, he heard the rice farmer and the millet farmer arguing nearby. He hurried over to offer his wise counsel.

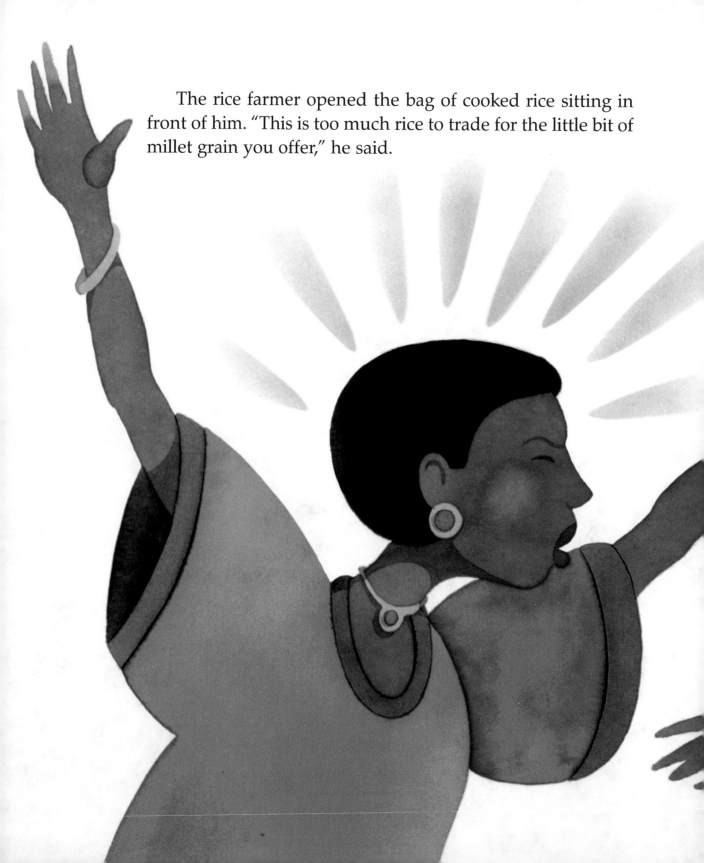

The rice farmer opened the bag of cooked rice sitting in front of him. "This is too much rice to trade for the little bit of millet grain you offer," he said.

"No, no, this is too much millet for the little bag of rice!" The millet farmer piled her creamy white cooked millet on a bright cloth. The two traders leaned toward each other, getting angrier with each word. They glared and waved their arms wildly! Their voices rose louder and louder.
Denden. DENDEN!

Ananse examined their wares. The cooked rice was plump and abundant. The heap of millet looked tasty. Ananse rubbed his belly. Without calling attention to his wisdom, Ananse helped the rice farmer by eating some of his rice so there would no longer be too much. Then he helped the millet farmer by eating some of the extra millet.

Now, when the farmers noticed Ananse's wise deed, did they thank him? They did not. They chased him out of the marketplace!

Too clever to be caught, Ananse made webs connecting the thatched roofs of the village houses and sneaked out of town unnoticed. Then he raced for home.

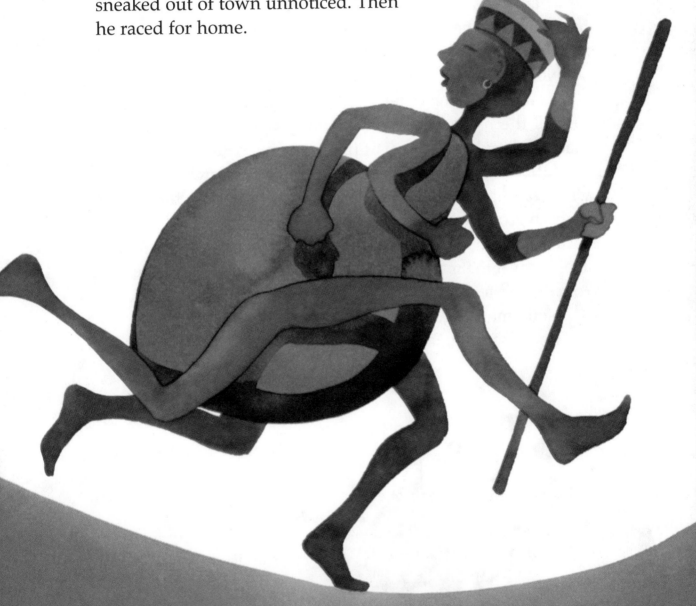

Panting, Ananse leaned against the palm tree that towered over his family's small hut, shaking his head.

How the farmers had mistreated him! People just didn't appreciate his nyansa. Ungrateful fools! Did they ever thank him for sharing his wisdom with them? For solving their problems? For spreading knowledge wherever he went? No! No! No!

Enough of being generous! Ananse decided. He would take back all the nyansa he'd given to the world. He'd put it in a calabash gourd and hide it at the top of his palm tree.

He looked across his family's farm. He watched his wife, Aso, working in her field of millet. He admired the field of calabash grown by his son, Ntikuma. It was green and vigorous, stuffed with gourds. Surely his young son wouldn't need to sell all of them at the market. Ananse saw Ntikuma poke his head up from behind a large calabash.

"Good morning, my son," Ananse said, smiling.

"Good morning, Father." Ntikuma glanced up from his weeding.

"Son," said Ananse, his eyes scanning the field, "I need a gourd in which to store my nyansa. So tell me, could you spare one of your calabashes?"

"Sure, Father," said Ntikuma with a smile. He jumped up and strode across the field, whistling.

Ananse rested in the shade of the palm. Just as he began to doze off, Ntikuma returned. "Where's the—" began Ananse.

"Here's a gourd, Father." Ntikuma held out a tiny calabash.

"That runt?" exclaimed Ananse. "Why, that stunted thing couldn't even hold the millet farmer's smarts! Son, I need a big gourd." Ananse stretched out his many long legs, showing Ntikuma the enormous size of the desired gourd.

"I'll try to find one," said Ntikuma, getting his digging stick. He set off across the field.

13

"That's a calabash!" exclaimed Ananse when his son returned, rolling a giant golden gourd. "It's bigger than big. It's a kokuroo calabash!" Ananse thumped it happily. "Thanks, Son."

"You're welcome." Ntikuma pointed at the hole in the gourd where the thick stem had been connected. "How are you going to get wisdom in there?"

Ananse picked up a palm frond from the ground, saying, "I'll sweep up the wisdom I've scattered here and there, leaving it for fools. Then I'll put it inside."

"I've never seen wisdom before," said Ntikuma, bright-eyed. "May I come along as you sweep?"

"You see it every day, Son. You live with me! You just don't recognize it." Ananse sighed. "You bring the calabash, all right?"

Ananse began by sweeping the family's one-room hut. He brushed under his bed, collecting the wisdom that had fallen off him while he dreamed. He swept under the table, picking up the snippets of genius that had dropped from his mouth during dinner conversation. He carried the palm frond outside, shook it in the opening of the gourd, and plugged the hole with a rag.

Next he cleaned the weedy area around the hut and brushed the twisting trail that led to the marketplace. Ntikuma followed behind, shoving, pulling, and rolling the unwieldy kokuroo calabash. "It looks nice where you've swept, Father," he huffed.

They followed the trail up a grassy hill to the village market. Wielding his palm frond, Ananse pushed his way between the tightly packed stalls and rushing shoppers. He quickly dusted between the heaps of fruits and vegetables, hoping to take back all the smart advice he'd offered so freely.

"Never seen you work before, Brother Ananse," said the weaver with surprise. "What's the occasion?"

Unwilling to risk sharing wisdom by speaking, Ananse simply waved his hand and moved on. He cleaned the entire market, except for the area where rice and millet were sold. He didn't want to save his knowledge of angry farmers chasing him.

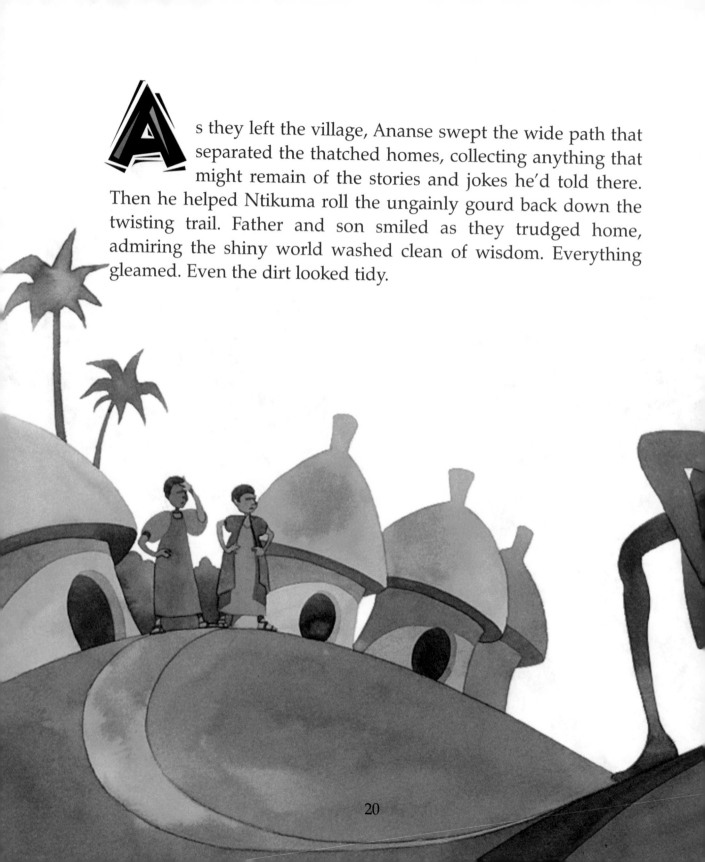

As they left the village, Ananse swept the wide path that separated the thatched homes, collecting anything that might remain of the stories and jokes he'd told there. Then he helped Ntikuma roll the ungainly gourd back down the twisting trail. Father and son smiled as they trudged home, admiring the shiny world washed clean of wisdom. Everything gleamed. Even the dirt looked tidy.

hen they reached the palm, Ntikuma pulled the rag out of the calabash and peered inside. "Wisdom looks a lot like dirt," he commented, disappointment in his voice.

"Of course, my son," answered Ananse. "All good things come from the soil of Africa. Wisdom is no different from rice or millet."

Ananse wrapped a cord around the calabash. "Hold the gourd steady, will you, Son? I want to put in the nyansa that I've stored in my head."

Ananse took a deep breath. He leaned forward, putting his mouth over the opening in the calabash. Then he breathed his wisdom into the gourd. He blew and blew until his face turned purple. He puffed a final gasp of nyansa, and all his knowledge went into the calabash. He didn't have a wise thought left in his head.

He quickly stuffed the rag into the hole before the wisdom could leak out. Then he looped the cord over his head and hung the kokuroo calabash in front of him. The weight of it made him wobble. Ntikuma steadied him and gave him a boost onto the palm.

Ananse began to climb very slowly. The big gourd stuck out so far in front of him that he could barely grip the smooth tree trunk.

"Father—" began Ntikuma.

"Not now, Son," Ananse barked. "I'm busy." He crawled slowly up the tree. The trunk became thinner and more slippery as he went up. Ananse held on by eight legs, then seven, six, five, four, three, two. When he was almost at the top, he dangled from the palm by one leg!

26

He swung and the calabash bumped him. *Pem so!* He fell down with a thud. *Paw!*

"Father, if you—" tried Ntikuma.

"Son, please, I'm trying to concentrate." Ananse struggled up the tree, then slid down. *Pem so paw!*

"The calabash, Father—" said Ntikuma.

Again Ananse went up and fell down. *Pem so paw!* Ntikuma helped his father up. "If you put the gourd on your back, you'll climb easily," he offered.

Ananse nodded and swung the gourd around. With it on his back, he easily scurried up the trunk. He sat at the top of the tree on a cushion of palm fronds, looking down at his son.

"Ntikuma is so young and already so smart!" Ananse shouted with pride. "I thought I carried all the nyansa of the world, but I didn't know how to carry the calabash. How could I have overlooked my son's wisdom?" Ananse took off the gourd, his head full of the new nyansa Ntikuma had taught him.

"No one can hoard all the wisdom of the world," Ananse yelled. He waved his son away from the palm tree. Then he pulled out the rag and tipped the kokuroo calabash off the top of the tree. *Crash!* The gourd broke and wisdom escaped, scattered by the winds to all the homes and paths of the world. *Tetsee!*

Ananse has the last word:
"Ene se nyanse obiara nyaa bie, na wo a wanko ho ntem no, ene 'kwasea."
"That is how everyone got wisdom, and anyone who did not get there in time is—excuse my saying so—a fool."

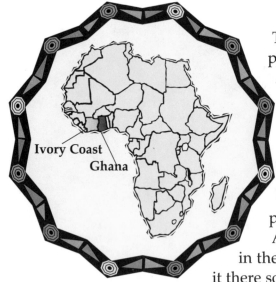

Ivory Coast
Ghana

The Akan are a large group of West African people, including the Asante (also spelled *Ashanti*) and the Fante. The language spoken by many people living in this area is also known as Akan. The Akan probably began to migrate to West Africa about 2,500 years ago from the dry areas of northern Africa, such as the Sahara. They settled in the region that is now Ghana and part of the Ivory Coast. The population of Ghana is 44 percent Akan.

According to a legend, the first Asante to arrive in the area emerged from a volcanic crater. He liked it there so much, he decided to stay.

The first settlements of the Asante were villages in which the houses were built close together. This was because the trees of the forest were too large to remove. Over the years, improvements in technology have made it possible to cut down the old rain forest trees. People who are concerned about the environment believe that human development of the rain forest is harming and even destroying many of the native plants and animals there.

The Asante empire was powerful because of its rich gold mines. European explorers in the early 1400s named the area the Gold Coast, and European traders began centuries of trade in gold and slaves.

Today, over 30 million people live in Ghana and the Ivory Coast. Some gold is still mined, as well as diamonds. Cocoa and lumber are important exports. Most of the inhabitants live and work on small farms.